LONDON • SYDNEY

This story is based on the traditional fairy tale,
Rapunzel, but with a new twist.
You can read the original story in
Hopscotch Fairy Tales. Can you make
up your own twist for the story?

First published in 2013 by
Franklin Watts
338 Euston Road
London
NW1 3BH

Franklin Watts Australia
Level 17/207 Kent Street
Sydney
NSW 2000

Text © Karyn Gorman 2013
Illustrations © Laura Ellen Anderson 2013

A CIP catalogue record for this book is available
from the British Library.

ISBN 978 1 4451 1630 3 (hbk)
ISBN 978 1 4451 1636 5 (pbk)

Series Editor: Melanie Palmer
Series Advisor: Catherine Glavina
Series Designer: Peter Scoulding

Printed in China

Franklin Watts is a division of
Hachette Children's Books,
an Hachette UK company.
www.hachette.co.uk

To the dream team –
you know who you are!
K.G.

Once upon a time, in Far Away land, the Prince of Pop was driving through the forest when he heard the most enchanting voice.

He was surprised to discover that the voice belonged to a fair maiden who lived in the highest tower of a dark castle.

The Prince could not see a way to reach the girl until he saw an old, wretched witch approach.

"Rapunzel, Rapunzel, let down your hair," called the witch. All of a sudden, a braid of golden locks fell from the window. The witch quickly climbed to the top.

That night the Prince approached the tower and said, "Rapunzel, Rapunzel, let down your hair."

Once again, the braid appeared
and the Prince began to climb up
until he reached the window.

"Who are you?"

Rapunzel screamed.

"I'm the Prince of Pop," replied the Prince. "I represent all of Far Away's top talent. I heard you sing and you shall be my next big star!"

Each night the Prince would visit Rapunzel in her tower to develop her act.

He coached her on her singing.

Instructed her on her dance.

And lectured her on

her "star appeal".

"You will make me millions," said the Prince. "But first we must free you from that awful witch."

Rapunzel looked doubtful, but she did want to be free.

The next night, the Prince returned
to free Rapunzel from the tower.
But when he called out for her,
she wasn't there.

17

In desperation, the Prince searched for his star all over town but she was nowhere to be found.

Then one day, as the Prince was passing by a recording studio, he tripped over something.

Far Out Fairy Tunes

The Prince followed the hair until he saw… "Rapunzel! I've been looking for you everywhere! Where have you been?" he screamed.

"I've been busy," said Rapunzel.
"I've been working on my
second album."

"But what about me?" spluttered the Prince. "What about my millions?"

"Sorry," shrugged Rapunzel. "But I've decided to go with another agent."

"But hey, thanks for helping me out," said Rapunzel.

The Prince was speechless.

And so, Rapunzel and her agent
the witch lived happily ever after.
And the Prince of Pop was left still
searching for his next big star.

Puzzle 1

Put these pictures in the correct order.
Which event do you think is most important?
Now try writing the story in your own words!

Choose the correct speech bubbles for each character. Can you think of any others? Turn over to find the answers.

Answers

Puzzle 1

The correct order is: 1c, 2a, 3e, 4d, 5f, 6b

Puzzle 2

Rapunzel: 2, 5

The witch: 3, 4

Prince of Pop: 1, 6

Look out for more Hopscotch Twisty Tales and Fairy Tales:

For more Hopscotch books go to:
www.franklinwatts.co.uk

*hardback